I Wish I Could Fly

by RON MARIS

GREENWILLOW BOOKS, NEW YORK

without permission in writing
from the Publisher,
Greenwillow Books, a division
of William Morrow & Co. Inc.,
105 Madison Avenue,
New York, N.Y. 10016.

Printed in Belgium ⊻

First American Edition

10 9 8 7 6 5 4 3 2 1

Library of Congress
Cataloging-in-Publication Data
Maris, Ron.   I wish I could fly.
Summary: Turtle wishes he could fly, dive,
climb, and run like other animals, but then he
realizes something he can do that they can't.
[1. Turtles—Fiction.   2. Animals—Fiction.
3. Individuality—Fiction]   I. Title.
PZ7.M338975Ib 1986   [E]   86-9797
ISBN 0-688-06654-2
ISBN 0-688-06655-0 (lib. bdg.)

FOR CATHERINE, JANE, JOANNE,
MICHAEL, SALLY, AND STEVEN

"Good morning, Bird."

"I wish I could fly like you."

CRASH! BANG!
WALLOP! CRUNCH!

"Hello, Frog."

"I wish I could dive like you."

FLOP! PLOP!
SPLUTTER! SPLASH!

"How are you, Squirrel?"

"I wish I could climb like you."

WIBBLE! WOBBLE!
WRIGGLE! ROCK!

"Good day, Rabbit."

"I wish I could run like you."

PUFF! PANT!
STAGGER! GASP!

"I can't fly like Bird,
 I can't dive like Frog,
 I can't climb like Squirrel,
 I can't run like Rabbit, but…"

"When it rains,
I don't get wet.
I'm **SNUG, WARM,
COSY,** and **DRY!**"

J M